BEYOND BORDERS

THE COALESCENCE OF PROSE AND POETRY

LORELA GARCIA CARPIO
LORAINE GARCIA ASAS

BEYOND BORDERS: The Coalescence of Prose and Poetry

by Lorela Garcia Carpio and
Loraine Garcia Asas

Illustrated by: Lauriane Rose G. Carpio

ISBN
Hardbound-978-621-495-237-3
Softbound/Paperback-978-621-495-266-3
PDF (read only)-978-621-495-267-0

Published by:
Poetry Planet Book Publishing House
Rosario, Pozzorubio, Pangasinan, Philippines
Registered under
National Library of the Philippines

DEDICATION

For Louisiane

and

Lauriane

PREFACE

This book, BEYOND BORDERS: The Coalescence of Prose and Poetry is another compilation of creative writing pieces in which the primary purpose is to introduce to the young readers an approach to the writing of 21st Century Literature where usual and ordinary life situations are reflected on the pages.

The coalescence of prose and poetry that the authors ventured to present in this book is deemed to provide a range of subjects where literature could be seen as a vehicle for the introduction of the use of vernacular language and the reintroduction of local color in short stories and unique rhyme schemes in poetry.

Through these lenses, it could be viewed that the authors wrote each piece of short story in the greatest extent of liberty in literary writing as they put on paper the daily spoken language rather than the formal language alongside the use of recognizable locale that adds vividness to the local color.

As for the contributed poetic pieces, it could be inferred that the authors intentionally exercised greater control about where the readers would place emphasis for decoding content and interpretation when dealing with a poem.

As a whole, this book, BEYOND BORDERS: The Coalescence of Prose and Poetry was conceived not only to serve as reference or pattern of young writers in their journey to creative writing but also as a significant memento of appreciation to people behind Poetry Planet for their unparalleled efforts to uphold literature and for their unwavering support to local writers.

-LG Carpio
and LG Asas

Table of Contents

PROSE

POETRY

Prose

I Concede

Lorela Garcia Carpio

"To love and win is the best thing. To love and lose, the second best."

-William Makepeace Thackeray

I stood in the barren living room as I searched from the four corners of it all her bitter-sweet smiles, her charming frowns...

I gazed at the sofa for a couple of minutes trying to find her in her usual position while scribbling stories on her laptop. I moved a few steps toward the dining room, tears rolling down my face as I desperately reminisced our birthdays, our anniversaries, our Valentines days, our Christmases and New Years together.

I went upstairs pausing by the door of our bedroom. I lit a cigarette and closed my eyes, picturing her before the mirror, combing the long brown hair cascading through her shoulders. I lifted an angel figurine displayed on top of her dresser and for the very first time saw what she inscribed with a red pentel pen on one of its wings: *"12/04/2000- I love you always."* I looked around the bedroom; got into the closet which still brings the scent of her favorite perfume.

I touched her dresses and blouses and skirts– all in purple and violet, lilac and magenta...black and white... Then suddenly, I laughed through my tears.

I hurriedly went downstairs, slammed the front door of the house, and got into the car. I suddenly heard, *"Daddy! Bye daddy!" "Bye Daddy!"* I brought my sight to the direction of the shouting and saw my little boy, Luigi riding on his bicycle. My eyes watered. It can't be. I sped off.

"Camila...Camila!!!..."

Gentle knocking at the door awoke me.

"You seemed to have a bad dream, sir. You were shouting. You were calling on Camila.

Anyway, sir, I'm Fricie, the nurse assigned to you. Here's your medicine, please take it," the nurse spoke while entering my room. She headed towards me and handed to me a capsule and a glass half-filled with water. She looked at me smilingly and asked, *"Who is Camila? Would you like me to call her for you?"*

I opted not to reply.

***

I zoomed my lenses to get a better shot of her. I couldn't catch her eyes but I could see her profile clearly.

Long brown hair gathered on the side, silky complexion, narrow shoulders, and slender body. She seems to be writing something on a notebook. She tilted her head slightly, as though searching for a certain vocabulary that had slipped off her mind.

The silver sand glistened through the sunlight as though crystals surrounding a goddess resting by the shore. The wind blew. Her long brown hair flew across her innocent face and she blew it back.

What a sight to behold! Perfect!

I reviewed from my camera if I was able to capture such a loveliest view.

She turned quickly. God! I saw those mysterious brown eyes that even in her sadness seem to smile. I can never forget her flashy aura, her nearly perfect-shaped nose and pronounced cheekbones...her lips.

But what I always remember about her features were her eyes...mysterious brown eyes that flashes a smile...I think even in the presence of pain. Those mysterious brown eyes that would haunt me forever.

"Sir Louie, you better take a rest now. I'll be back at 2:30 p.m. for another dose of your medicines. It's okay if you don't want to tell me who Camila is." She said with an embarrassed smile.

I shook my head.

***

"Why don't you pursue a teaching job? I mean, English teacher, that's perfect for you," I started a conversation one time when I saw

her seriously brainstorming for another short story to write.

"I had already thought of that but I feel I'm never into it."

"So, you're more into writing than teaching!" I commented. *"They said writers were just trying to repair themselves…to heal themselves."*

She gazed at me as though examining what I meant with what I said.

"Maybe they're right," she said as she brought her attention back to what she was writing, *"because writers feel fuller when they can weave stories out of their life's episodes, even if the story is not entirely true and even if they are really just fabricating."*

I lit a cigarette. I inhaled deeply, blowing the smoke in a steady stream.

"When you teach, you touch lives," I insisted.

"That's true. As true as when you write, you engrave your name to eternity."

She was the type who accepts one's opinions then insists on her own.

***

"Good afternoon, sir Louie," Frincie, the nurse uttered as she entered my room.

. I raised my right hand as though to welcome her.

"Its 2:30, it's time for your medicines."

"Thanks."

When she has left, I all the more felt the void in me. I remembered Camila and how she had left me; frozen in time...too soon...just as when my love for her was blooming.

Drowsiness. The colors and images around me gradually faded. Effects of the medicines I had taken. Effects maybe.

***

So, what is better off, one who shares love long enough to see which parts inevitably fade or one who loses his love when it is still pristine?

It was nearing twilight when I went to meet Mildred in her apartment somewhere in the north.

"Did she know you're here?' she inquired welcoming me with warm kisses in my nose till our lips met for a couple of seconds.

"I don't think so. I said I have a photo exhibit to attend to."

"So, how long would you be staying?"

"I can stay so long as you want me to stay," I replied as she held my gaze on her.

"Did she ever suspect we're together every time you disappear?" she asked.

"I doubt. I do not know. Maybe." I lit a cigarette. I inhaled deeply and blew the smoke out from the side of my mouth.

"But what if she discovers?" she asked rather anxiously.

I drew here near me and she buried her face on my chest.

"Relax, my dearest Mildred. Believe me, she would never figure this out," I said

trying so hard to console her though I knew from within that I was more than lying.

I started to kiss Mildred on her forehead, on her hair, on her face, on her lips... We held each other's arms wrapped tightly and went straight into her bedroom.

***

12:45 a.m.

I still lay awake.

I was blank, as though I was thinking of nothing.

I turned to kiss Mildred who was already asleep for hours.

My Mildred. My first love.

Whenever I'm with her, it's like I am plunged backward when it was only the two of us then. It's like I am drawn closer to those times and places long left behind.

Mildred. I can't afford to lose her again. She left her husband for me. I can also leave my wife and son for her.

I closed my eyes as though attempting to escape from this mess where I foolishly but satisfyingly dragged myself into.

***

"When could I see that you're not writing?"

She shrugged her right shoulder and went on scribbling over her old scrap notebook.

"I have loved writing ever since. It's hard to turn away from who, rather uhmm, I mean from 'what' you love."

She was like talking to scrap notebook; not giving me even a sudden look.

I was perplexed. *Did she mean something or anything by that?*

"So, what's the theme of your latest story in the making?" I asked while drawing closer to her at the sofa.

She gazed at me, maybe trying to catch my eyes. I bent as though reaching for the ash tray on top of the center table then, I lit a cigarette and blew smoke in chains.

"This is about first love. I would like to keep my story hanging by leaving to the readers the extent of truth behind the line – First love never dies," she said while looking at me smilingly.

"A cliché. A literal stereotype, I would say if I were your reader,"
I commented trying to make a sarcastic remark but I felt that my voice squeaked.

"So, you don't believe that first love never dies?" she queried trying to catch my eyes again.

I composed myself very well and gave her the reply that I think she wanted– *"I don't believe,"* I said with such an ounce of emphasis and I extinguished my cigarette on the ash tray as though ending our conversation.

Her forehead crinkled; then she smiled. I cupped her left hand with my hands and pressed the ring on her finger. I felt her hand quiver.

Didn't Camila figure out what was happening?

Didn't she get any hint of it? If she did, why was it that she never confronted me? Maybe she knew nothing. Or she was just damn good in faking. Maybe. She was good.

I gripped her hand feeling sorry for her. She gripped my arm, pressing it harder. Her grip grew tighter and stronger. I felt like she'll never loosen her grip anymore. Never. I tried to move my arm but the grip grew firm and tighter.

"Oh, I'm very sorry, sir. I'm just checking on your blood pressure."
It was Frincie, the nurse. Her face registered a very apologetic expression.

"160 over 100. That's a high BP sir. You need to relax."

I searched for the clock hanging on the wall. 3:30 a.m.

I was like craving for a cigarette, but there was no way I can have it again.

***

Camila.

She was but one of the many women in my life. A playmate, somehow, of my rather romantic heart. The hardest thing is that I never knew she would be the last. The one who would defeat me in this game.

Camila.

She has the memory of a love, too good to be true. She taught me how to love–truly; so true that it would be difficult to love again.

Camila...

The past came ever sharper into focus, bringing me into a retrospect of scenes that have never faded in my irresolute mind.

***

"I'm very sorry this had to happen. I never wanted us to end this way."

I felt surprised by the words I uttered. Was it me who was talking?

"You don't have to be sorry, Louie. Of all people, I should be the one to understand you best. It's hard to find the right person, isn't it? Someone you could love without losing yourself," she said while throwing inside a travelling bag a few of her clothes and Luigi's.

I lit a cigarette but immediately tossed it out of the window.

She gazed at me as though inquiring for my sentiments. I cannot stand her gazing at me. I cupped my hands and blew into them.

"I'm sorry…I mean…Mildred and I…

We're very sorry to have caused you this pain."

She turned to look at me. She took both of my hands; kissed me quickly in my lips and said, *"I believe each person gets to truly love just once. We may have loved many others along the way but as the days eluded by, we will realize that there will only be one true love for us. You have lost Mildred once, could you bear losing her again?"* Her voice was breaking.

I felt my face reddened.

I looked away feeling cornered by her question.

I reached for my cigarette pack and lit a cigarette. One. Two. Three. Four. Until all the sticks were consumed.

I looked at them. Teary. Oh Camila, and my son Luigi.

My God! Please help me!

"So…so…uhmmm…I mean…" I couldn't get the words to say.

"So, game over. It's hard to compete with first love…" she said with a bitter-sweet smile. My God! That smile almost killed me– flashy in the presence of pain.

"So, you're setting me free?" I didn't know if it was right of me to have asked that. But what should I say?

"I'm not setting you free, Louie. You have always been free. I never had you, can't you see?"

Every word she uttered sank unto me; boulders of quagmire reverie, a thousand rusty spears striking my being…gradually pulling me to death.

She cupped my face with her both hands trying hard to capture my eyes. She kissed me on my forehead…on my nose…in my lips and said, *"Thanks for everything."*

I waited until she finally dropped her arms and then I pulled her back, kissed her desperately. I couldn't let go. Why? The hell! I couldn't let go…

My son, Luigi crinkled his forehead trying hard to decode what was happening.

She finally pushed me and headed to the door while holding Luigi tightly in his arm.

I could see her face in the moonlight, streaked with tears.

"Daddy! Bye daddy!" "Bye Daddy!"

Luigi…Camila…

I called their names in silence.

***

The sunlight beaming from the windows welcomed me in my new awakening. I looked at the wall clock. 8:22 a.m.

It has been thirty-nine years.

Thirty-nine long years that I have been searching for Camila and my son. I was blinded by such an intoxicating first love that I let genuine love slip away. I have nothing and no one but myself to blame. I let our years of marriage disappear in the mist.

There were times that I was thinking of finally finding Camila. But, perhaps the almost four decades of my search wasn't enough...yet.

And what if I finally find Camila? What would I tell her?

Hi Camila! Do you still remember me? Louie Aragon, the dashing photographer who captured your heart fifty-one years back?

Tell me. What would I tell her?

Hi Camila. Can you still remember me? I'm Louie Aragon, your husband who loves you so much? What an irony! Better, your husband whom you had loved so much...

Tell me. Would those desperate words be fine?

And what is the use of finding her again?

To win her back, when I turn eighty?

***

"Good morning, Sir Louie." Frincie, the nurse.

"Just to inform you that you are okay for discharge this afternoon as per your signed request," she said smilingly. She went on, *"The laboratory tests were all done and the specialist shall be talking with you later about the results."*

I shook my head.

***

I packed in a small, old bag the few clothes I had brought to the hospital. My two days of confinement for the purpose of observation felt like eternity.

I closed the door of my room and walked slowly through the lobby, looking at each door, reading the room numbers and the names of the patients confined in the respective rooms.

108.

Pepito S. Legazpi

107.

Zenaida B. Lucena

106.

Angelica T. Cabrera

105.

Camila V. Aragon

***

Camila V. Aragon. Camila V. Aragon

Could it be her? Camila Valderama Aragon.

No. It couldn't be her.

But what if it was her?

I slowly got hold of the door knob. My hand was trembling. Suddenly, I was like frozen in time, still holding the door knob, I cannot manage to move in any way.

"Excuse me, sir. Are you going to visit the patient here?"

Still with my hand frozen on the door knob, I looked back. Approaching me was a very pretty young lady whom I think was in her teens. My hand slipped from the knob. I smiled then I nodded as though to affirm her.

"Do you know my grandma?" she exclaimed while opening the door.

***

My God!

My ever-dearest Camila!

Long, silver-gray hair gathered in a low pony tail, wrinkled face, and sagging skin. Time had changed her a lot, physically.

But it was still her.

Camila. My beloved Camila.

She nailed her gaze on me as I was left frozen again near the door. She smiled. How could I ever forget that smile? That smile that flashes even in the presence of pain.

Camila!

I couldn't stop my arms from reaching out and enclosing her in my sincerest embrace.

She cupped my face with her hands and drew back.

"Get out of here! Get lost! You never had me! You never had me! Only Louie! Only Louie! Only Louie!"

I tightened my grip on her hands but she was very strong like a warrior trying to be freed from captivity; like a pent-up volcano that had been dormant for a hundred years; like a slave trying to be freed from bondage...

I tightened my grip all the more but I felt like I was losing strength.

The young lady called for the nurses to assist in calming down her grandmother. The nurses came and gave Camila shot of tranquilizers. It was only then that she was calmed.

The young lady turned to me and spoke in a very low voice, *"I am very sorry sir. According to daddy Luigi, grandma is suffering from dementia."*

***

Grandma is suffering from dementia.

Suffering from dementia.

Suffering from dementia.

The voice kept echoing in the stillness of my being.

Thirty-nine years.

Thirty-nine long years.

All those years, I didn't get rid of her clothes, nor any of her things, even her handwritten story notes. Nothing. But it's clear that everything about her had gotten rid of me. I suddenly laughed through my tears.

For always, I'd stood in front of her closet. I'd gaze for hours at her beautiful clothes– dresses and blouses and skirts– all in purple and violet, lilac and magenta...black and white...

At times, I'd stand in front of the mirror and imagine her asking me if her clothes fit her perfectly.

Time and again, the angel figurine seemed to look at me with such a questioning gaze.

I just laugh through my tears.

Camila.

My ever-precious Camila.

She was such a great writer. She was able to show that even tragic love stories could sometimes have happy endings, like mine.

***

Cancer of the lungs.

Stage 3 or Stage 4.

It does not matter anymore.

The truth is I have never been afraid to die.

The truth is: I told myself that I will battle with death so long as there is time.

Now that I knew that I have never lost Camila, there is one clear thought that glitters through: I'm ready to die.

Even now.

With love, I concede to death.

Back to Square One

Lorela Garcia-Carpio

"You don't find love, it finds you. It's got a little bit to do with destiny, fate, and what's written in the stars."

-Anais Nin

What if you don't believe in love? Then someone teaches you how... Then you fall in love for that 'someone'...and you started to believe...Oooppppsss..."

A pothole on the road had nearly caused my motorcycle to get off balance. The long road that was full of potholes for years had been causing so much of annoying and toilsome travel to my workplace.

The scorching heat of the sun has become a little difficult to withstand; a number of tricycles passing by had been creating a thick fountain of smoke and dust which cause either coughing or sneezing to passers by. It was quarter to one in the afternoon and the students, mostly high schoolers, were heading back to the nearby public school for their afternoon classes.

"What if you don't believe in love? Then someone teaches you how... Then you fall in love for that 'someone'...and you started to believe in love. But what if..."Oooppppsss...My new Pilot..."

My pen which I slid into the left pocket of my pants fell off the ground. Too bad, the more that I'm trying to be so much careful about that pen, the more that it finds way to get dropped.

I got off my motorcycle, picked up my Pilot ballpen and put it inside the pocket of my backpack.

Five minutes before one o'clock.

I rode back on my motorcycle and sped off.

***

"What if you don't believe in love? Then someone teaches you how... Then you fall in love for that 'someone'...and you started to believe in love. But what if that someone is not supposed to love you, only to teach you?"

"So, this will be the central thought of the free verse poem that you are going to do as an enrichment activity. You may have your outputs submitted on or before February 3."

"Do you have anything to clarify about your learning task?"

"None sir," the students answered in chorus.

***

The observation class went very successfully, as usual. The meticulous observers from our department said that they were impressed with my Literature class and more so, with my strategies. They commended the flow of the lesson and most of all they found my springboard for the poetry writing enrichment task as a very creative approach.

In short, I aced the class observation with a bang! I went home happily with such a pride in my heart.

***

I parked my motorcycle and headed to the door.

The usual sight of my apartment unit welcomed me.

Dusty floor and furniture, coffee mug and plates on the sink, stinking frying pan...

I'm not surprised anymore. This has been life for me for almost twelve years.

I dumped my backpack on the dusty center table and plunged my body heavily on the equally dusty sofa.

"Sir JP!... sir JP!..."

I was awakened by the voice calling my name from the outside.

I looked at the wall clock to inquire for the time. 4:24

"4:24?" I wondered in a while. I reached for my cellphone from my backpack, looked into it to verify the time.

"Sir JP!... sir JP!..." the calling went on.

"7:45," I whispered to myself while heading lazily to the door.

"Spaghetti for you, sir."

I did not move.

I just felt the plate touched my chest. It was then that I seemed to be back to reality.

I glided my eyes on her from head to foot. A woman perhaps in her mid-twenties, in heavy make-up, dark-red lipstick, fake eyelashes, lavishly curled long blonde hair, wearing a red stiletto, black micro-mini skirt and red spaghetti strap top...holding a plate of spaghetti.

I wrinkled my forehead and tilted my head to the right.

"Spaghetti for you, sir! Birthday po ng nanay ko."

I wrinkled my forehead all the more and tilted my head to the left.

"I'm Felicity. We just moved here this morning...in the unit next to yours. The neighbors told me that you are Sir JP! So, is everything okay now? Aren't you going to take this?" she asked as she pouted her lips to point to the plate of spaghetti. *"Birthday po ng nanay ko!"* she repeated.

"I think this would be good for a dinner. I doubt it if you were able to cook your food. Your lights are still off up to this time, so don't tell me you were able to cook with the lights off."

Getting irritated by her too much talking, I took the plate from her.

"Thank you," she exclaimed with sarcasm.

"Thanks," I replied with embarrassment.

***

"So, can you please share any realization that you got from the story?" Yes, Rose Ann!"

"Sir, I realized that the story shares the same philosophy with Sarah Ban Breathnach in terms of lessons in life– that the greatest secret to living a happy life is the realization that everything is created in our minds before it manifests itself in the outer world; that we must believe it before we can see it."

"Very good! Who else would like to answer?"

Several students expressed their answers. Honestly, I could hardly connect with everything else that they shared. To my mind, everything about love and life is indeterminate …

***

I got home by around 5:15 in the afternoon.

While heading to the gate, I noticed a woman taking a load of clothes from the somewhat long wire clothesline. I glided my eyes on her from head to foot. A woman perhaps in her mid-twenties, with her long black hair held in a low pony tail. I cannot see her face very clearly from a little distance but all that I can see was a trace of simplicity. Her get-up– loose mocha-colored shirt and a seemingly faded black jogging pants.

I noticed that she wasn't wearing slippers.

My eyes were glued on her for a long while. I was still there, standing blankly when she approached me.

"Hi, Sir JP. Good afternoon!"

My forehead wrinkled. I did not speak.

"Felicity... remember?" she exclaimed while waving her hand nearly in front of my face. I hardly realize that my eyes were still glued on her. She turned away quickly leaving me like a statue riding on a motorcycle in front of the gate.

***

The usual sight of my apartment unit welcomed me.

Dusty floor and furniture, coffee mug and plates on the sink, stinking frying pan, ash tray full of cigarette butts, books scattered on the sofa...

I'm not surprised anymore. Same old scenery, but getting worse.

I picked the books and placed them on the dusty center table. I also dumped my backpack there and plunged my body heavily on the equally dusty wooden sofa.

"Sir JP!... sir JP!..."

I was awakened by the voice calling my name from the outside.

I looked at the wall clock to inquire for the time. 4:24.

"4:24?" I wondered in a while. *"Ah, why do I always forget to buy batteries for my wall clock?"* I reached for my cellphone from my backpack and looked into it to verify the time.

"Sir JP!... sir JP!..." the calling went on.

"7:19," I whispered to myself while heading lazily to the door.

"Sir, I just came to bring here your clothes. I got them off from the clothesline. It's already night time and besides, the rain is starting to fall."

I glided my eyes on her from head to foot.

A woman perhaps in her mid-twenties, in heavy make-up, dark-red lipstick, fake eyelashes, lavishly curled long blonde hair, wearing a silver high heeled shoes, silver micro-mini skirt and black spaghetti strap top...holding a bunch of my clothes.

I blankly took my clothes from her, unable to speak at the moment.

"Thank you," she spoke sarcastically as she walked away.

"Thanks," I replied shyly.

***

Days went on...I also went on with my life mechanically. I was just like a toy robot operated by batteries. I dealt with my life in such a hazy direction. I just lived for myself. I've been living this kind of life for so long that I do not know any other way to live my life anymore.

"Sir JP!... sir JP!..."

I was awakened by the voice calling my name from the outside.

I looked at the wall clock to inquire for the time. 4:24

"4:24?" I shook my head. *"Tomorrow I will buy a dozen of batteries for my wall clock."* I reached for my cellphone from my backpack and looked into it to verify the time.

"Sir JP!... sir JP!..." the calling went on.

"8:50," I was telling to myself while heading dizzily to the door.

"Sir, I know it's already late at night," she started to explain as she looked at her wristwatch. *It's already 8:50. But I'm getting worried because I had not seen you for a couple of days...I'm worried that something bad may have happened to you. I have not seen your motorcycle out of the terrace since last Wednesday," she narrated without hesitation.*

I glided my eyes on her from head to foot. She seemed to be in her mid-twenties, with her long black hair held in a low pony tail. In this very close proximity, I was able to gaze at her face very clearly. Her hazel-brown eyes were flashy and vividly beautiful, her nose was finely-shaped, her cheeks were glowing even without make up, and her lips were very much inviting even without lipstick. Just like before, all that I can see was a trace of simplicity. She was in her very simple loose white t-shirt and dark brown jogger pants.

"Sir!" she broke my silence while waving her hand in front of my face.

I was brought back to real time.

"I brought you noodles and sandwiches; I hope you will take these. I presumed you're sick," she uttered smilingly.

I got the tray holding a bowl of noodles and sandwiches from her. My eyes were still glued on her face. *"Uhmmm...I just caught flu and high fever for a couple of days... but uhmmm...I'm getting okay now,"* I spoke timidly.

"Well, that's very nice to hear, sir."

"Maybe I can go to work on Monday," I muttered.

"You mean, tomorrow? It's Monday tomorrow."

"Ah, yes. Would you mind to come in?" I mumbled.

"No, Thanks sir. I have to run an errand for my mother. Maybe tomorrow I'll come in," she said with a teasing smile.

I smiled back.

***

Okay class, your activity for our Literature session for today which is to be accomplished until Wednesday in your respective groups, is to make an electronic poster about this quote from Rumi: "Your task is not to seek love, but merely to seek and find all the barriers within yourself that you have built against it."

My usual day in school ended with a usual feeling of tiredness and monotony. I went home immediately trying to escape from the rain that seemed to fall.

I knew the usual sight of my apartment unit will welcome me.

Dusty floor and furniture, coffee mug and plates on the sink, stinking frying pan, ash tray full of cigarette butts, books scattered on the sofa... There's no way it would change. I know that.

***

"Did I get into the wrong unit?" I asked myself as I stood like a statue in front of the door. Before me was a sight of a well-swept floor and well-arranged furniture. I slowly moved into the kitchen area where I saw that the coffee mugs, plates and utensils were all well-placed on a dish drying rack. I blew a very little smile into the air.

"Sir JP!... sir JP!..."

My state of shock was broken by the voice calling my name from the outside.

"Sir JP!... sir JP!..."

I looked at the wall clock to check on the time.

4:24.

I shook my head in dismay. I always forget about the batteries.

"I hope sir, you won't take it against me...I entered your unit and did the 'brigada'...I mean the clean-up drive," she said with a big smile on her face.

Standing by the door was Felicity. I glided my eyes on her from head to foot... Heavy make-up, dark-red lipstick, fake eyelashes, lavishly curled long blonde hair, silver stiletto, black micro-mini skirt and red sleeveless top...

I didn't know that I was staring at her for quite a while.

"I wish you would feel even better with the cleaned-up house. You were getting sick because your house had never known how to clean itself," she broke the silence. She tilted

her head and smiled as she turned and walked away.

"Thanks," I replied. I didn't know if she heard it.

For quite a long while, it seemed that I was brought to a different world. The feeling deep inside was so strange that I knew it wasn't only the apartment unit had undergone a sort of change; somehow, a strange feeling had been creeping into my veins. It was something that I had known and felt before. I paused for a moment trying hard to decode that feeling; and I decided that whatever happens, I have to dismiss that strange feeling.

I lifted my left arm to inquire for the time from my wristwatch.

"6:22," I whispered to myself. The sky then was growing dark and the thick black clouds were hinting a heavy rainfall. I know it would be a long night of pondering for me.

***

I was awakened by the heavy downpour. As if by impulse, I looked at the wall clock to check on the time. "*4:24*," I said to myself; quite aware that the time wasn't right. So, I reached for my cellphone to inquire from it. "*4:24*," I said to myself smilingly. I felt a little surge of awe in my heart; after perhaps being used to a more than a hundred times of inquiring from my non-functional wall clock, it is only now that the time had gone exact with reality.

I wished that there will be an announcement for the suspension of classes but the early morning TV news will be by 5:00 so I opted for the meantime to make a cup of coffee to relieve the cold.

The sound of a vehicle that seemed to stop by the gate got my attention. I ran toward the window to see what that was about. I saw Felicity got off the taxi. I held my gaze on her from a distance.

I tried to focus my eyes on her from top to toe… I cannot see her heavy make-up anymore. Her dark-red lipstick seemed to have been erased; her fake eyelashes seemed to have been gone. But I know that it was Felicity– in her lavishly curled long blonde hair that is now messed up. Her black micro-mini skirt and black sleeveless top was covered with a gray knitted cardigan… She ran fast through the heavy rain holding her silver stiletto in her hand.

No announcement concerning class suspension came. I hurriedly prepared myself for the rainy day's work. With my rain coat, I got into my motorcycle and looked back at my apartment unit; with its door wide open, I could clearly see the nonfunctional wall clock.

"*4:24*," I uttered to myself.

I brought my glance back into the direction of the gate. I saw Felicity coming in; holding a plastic of *pan de sal* in her right hand and a floral umbrella in her left hand… I can't help but stare at her profile from head to toe.

Her long black hair was held in a low pony tail. Her hazel-brown eyes were flashy and vividly beautiful. Her nose was finely-shaped. Her cheeks were glowing; even more beautiful without make up. Her lips were better off without lipstick. Just like before, all that I can see was a trace of simplicity. Her usual casual get-up– black jogger pants and light gray t-shirt even made her youthful and simply amazing.

She saw me staring at her. She stopped for a while looking at me. Our gazes locked. I surrendered.

"Ah…uhmmm… pan de sal for a rainy morning," I said with a rather reluctant smile.

She smiled back. *"Take some, sir,"* she exclaimed as she raised the plastic of bread to me.

"No, thanks," I said and then I went heading for school. It was already almost a half-way drive when I remembered the wide-open door of my unit. Opting to come back, I inquired for the time from my wrist watch. *"6:53,"* I sighed and just went on.

***

My usual Literature class drifted with the heavy downpour that had started since four o'clock. By around ten thirty, our school's covered path walk was already flooded due to the rain water that added up to the rising flood water caused by high tide. With that situation ensued an announcement that classes in the municipality was thereby suspended. Thanks to the prompt announcement of the good mayor! In an instant, the whole campus was cleared of students and teachers. I was left alone. I opted to stay in the faculty room.

***

In silence, I tried hard to examine myself. What had seemed to change within me? I knew that a mystical feeling had started to evade my emptiness but I can't figure it out. Or maybe, I just wanted not to know it. I tried to keep my mind busy so I got a bundle of students' output and intended to check at least a few. Two hours had elapsed and I had not moved even a single paper from the bundle. I decided to go home. The flood was gradually creeping into our school's covered court. It was no surprise anymore for me.

***

I got home after a less than an hour drive. The rain had stopped for a while but the flood water seemed to be rising. I hurriedly approached my apartment unit; its door was still wide open just as I left it. The sight of a well-swept floor and well-arranged furniture and the well-kept kitchen area delighted me. I smiled and blew into the air.

I sought for the batteries from my backpack then went straight into the wall clock.

1:00.

Alas! It's already functioning.

With a smile, I placed the batteries on top of the center table. I decided to take a rest on my wooden sofa.

***

A sudden calling from the outside awakened me.

"Sir JP!... sir JP!..."

I looked at the wall clock to check on the time.

"4:24," I sighed.

I prepared myself for this encounter that I had waited to happen. I gathered all my confidence before I head to the door.

I know...it was Felicity.

For the first time after many years of isolation and solitude, I recognized from the core of my heart that I am alive...that I am capable of happiness...that it could be true that one day, love would just be knocking at my door...

I smiled and blew into the air before I opened the door.

Standing by the door was Felicity.

I glided my eyes on her from head to foot... Simple make-up, red lipstick, long black straight hair gathered in a low pony tail, elegant floral dress partnered with a white high-heeled shoes. Her hazel-brown eyes caught my gaze. She smiled shyly.

"Sir, I just came to bid you goodbye," she spoke.

I was surprised. I did not expect her words.

"My boyfriend, an old businessman who used to be my customer in the club offered me to live with him in Manila. He got the approval of my mother, and I also agreed...for practical reasons sir, you know..."

I did not utter any word. I'm battling with reality and make-believe. In fantasy, I have seen myself with Felicity. How I wished that I was still asleep; and that later on she would be sweetly calling my name.

"Sir, there are extra batteries in your drawer for your wall clock," she mumbled as she gave me a quick smack on my lips.

I don't know why I couldn't move. I was stuck. I couldn't understand what was taking place. All that I know was that I was brought back to square one.

Bounded

Loraine Garcia Asas

"Unrequited love does not die; it's only beaten down to a secret place where it hides, curled and wounded."
-Elle Newmark

She was on a hurry. She looked at her watch and took a quick browse on the pages. She fixed her things and she was on her way walking through the hallway when she remembered something. She quickly turned her back and walked a little faster. She was shocked. I could sense that she feels a sudden ache in her right shoulder. When she looked up, she met my gaze. In our strange silence, our eyes locked. Before she could take her eyes away from me, in an instance I smiled at her, not knowing, she would smile back at me.

"I'm sorry."

She just nodded her head.

"You are –"

"I would be late."

She interrupted and started to walk and searched for her next classroom. She knew I was right there walking after her, but she managed not to get affected.

It was indeed an opportunity that knocked on me. And I was thankful for that chance of having such proximity with the girl I longed to meet.

I could always see her passing through the hallway of my old room. I was always there in the corridor waiting to see her and wishing that somehow, she could give back my friendly greetings. But those were just my secret wishes. No one knew I always failed, and inside me, I was barely wounded.

She was the pretty smart girl everybody loved and cared the most; everyone adored, and I was so fond of her. But all I could do was just suit myself as I secretly stared at her from a distance. Just by simply seeing her could make and complete my day.

She was so close, but it seemed she was beyond my reach. Yes, she was bound to be beyond my reach. I could not even talk with her.

I envied those who had the chance to come closer to her.

When she saw me, she would just look at me. Then, she would look on the other side leaving an impression that she didn't care. Somehow, I understood her. Who would care for a guy like me who was so hard-headed and ill-tempered?

One day, I thought an angel came to meet my way. I was standing in the corridor of our classroom while waiting for the next subject, and as usual, waiting her coming. To glance at her face for a moment could make me feel satisfied. It was enough to complete my day.

But that chance of finally meeting her knocked me off. I was right. An angel came wearing a captivating smile, walking through my way that I happily thought that her smile was for me. But I was just mistakenly surprised. She only passed through my way and met up with somebody else. She was somebody's angel.

I had the chance of glancing closely at her face. But I felt a harsh squeeze in my heart. I saw that she was splendidly pretty. I saw how her face glowed as she happily smiled. But that smile was not for me. It was for someone. It was intended for the man walking behind me.

***

“I need to go… I would be late.”

She said and turned her back and started to walk away.

“I’m sorry...”

I muttered as I followed her. She just simply looked at me and I was left behind.

I didn’t feel sorry for loving her. I didn’t feel sorry for confiding her that I love her. I felt sorry for the silence that was between us. I felt sorry because I didn’t know what that silence meant.

Was it wrong to love her? Or did loving her mean wrong knowing she was loved by me?

***

I kept on asking myself, ‘When can love be wrong?’ I believe each person can go on loving anyone as per his or her feelings. However, expecting for that love to be reciprocated is another side of the story. I really don’t know if I should rest my case.

"Good morning, class!"

"Good morning, ma'am Rubio!"

Her life went to its normality, while I was left... still puzzled.

Vindicated

Loraine Garcia Asas

"The hardest part of losing someone isn't having to say goodbye, but rather learning to live without them; always trying to fill the void, the emptiness that's left inside your heart when they go."

-SD

"Hello?

Who's on the line?

Hel – lo?"

The sound of the end call cut her dialogue.

One message received.

"May I know who you are?"

Sudden pain engulfed my heart as I pressed the letters of my name.

She was one of the many acquaintances I had and one of the few girls I admired...not just because of her adoring face but much more of her awesome traits. She could be anybody's dream girl, but she was not aware of that.

For me, she was a friend, and I knew I was a friend for her too. If not, why would she spare some of her precious time because of my insipidity?

She was more than just a simple friend. Nobody knew about my stupidity except her. She even knew how dumb I was.

I met her by chance, a mere coincidence that apparently, I was the cause. I introduced myself and struck my first conversation with her. I got interested with her, thus I tried to befriend her. It was as if I was a teenager, gathering information to those who knew her. But it took some time before she permitted, still I was glad. She didn't disclose anything so easily, maybe because she didn't know me that much. The fact that we didn't see each other frequently because of works and priorities.

Though I didn't know more about her, I began to like her deeply. Before it started as a joke, I knew I really like her. And I just couldn't suit myself with the little things I knew about her.

Before I knew I became too hasty, I was dealing with the moment of telling her the way I could see her. She believed it was just a big joke. She was not surprised either. I didn't know how I could convince her that she was special to me.

I tried harder to convince her – telling I wanted to court her. Right there and then, she permitted me to know her answer. I was rejected. Though she told me she considered me as a friend, still I was rejected.

Then, our friendship turned silent. It felt like she was avoiding me. Every time we've seen each other, it was as if we were total strangers. There were casual conversations and it all ended there.

I haven't realized earlier what I have done. Maybe I was hurt when I felt rejection. Maybe what I have done was a way of saving my personal ego.

I saw her in a crowd. I ignored her – knowing she used to ignore me too. I thought she would get envious or jealous knowing I was right there talking with someone – not just simply talking, but it was more of a flirting. She was not affected. She didn't even bother to look.

I've tried to win her attention, wishing she could notice me. Yes, she noticed me and I left her a thought and impression that later had put me in regrets.

Through her, I have created a vague attachment with someone I knew as her friend. We spent some time talking and knowing each other. No farther elaboration of what she really meant to me, because I knew it was quite impossible to work out whatever intention I had for her because she was already taken. But to my utter surprise, she responded to my little tempting.

As a new friendship started to bloom out, I was not aware that I was slowly losing her. I tried really hard to get rid of her from my system. I tried to ignore her and what I felt for her.

When I was denied, I thought she was too inconsiderate. I have told her everything that a girl would love to hear, but she didn't give me a chance. It was all I knew 'til the moment we met again.

Her face was void of any emotion as she met my gaze. But she can still laugh and smile with our fellow friends. She was what she used to be and was not even bothered by my presence, leaving me a hint that she didn't care at all. I felt I was a total stranger.

It pained me knowing I could never change the impression she had about me – that no matter how hard I tried to put things back the way they used to be, I can no longer win her trust because of my insincerity.

She knew my last break-up. I confided to her almost everything, except for the part that it was because of her. I didn't know her impression about me would bring me into a realization that I fell so easily – that I was never serious because of the not so few relationships that I have been through. I could not blame her for that thought.

I was wrong when I thought she didn't give me the chance – for she had given me enough time. If I could just bring back the same things as before, I should have proven to her my real intention. Truly, words were not enough to win her heart.

I have just shown her how insincere I was. Because I have tried to save my pride and personal ego, I dealt with a vengeance that later had punished me.

She was right when she said I fell so easily – I fell for her so easily back then in our first meeting.

I wished I just suited myself with the friendship she once extended to me, than to end up here craving for the same closeness I could never have again. I haven't told and proven to her how much I love her, but everything we have had changed.

I waited for her reply, but there was none.

The girl who happened to be my friend is now gone. Though I know she is just around...

Poetry

She

Loraine Garcia Asas

She counts the days
'Til I come home
She jumps from bed
When she hears my voice
She smiles at me and tells me
She waits for me to come home.

She asks me to carry her
Buy her favorite candy from the store.
She asks me to play the music
And she sings her favorite song.

She likes me to cuddle her
And to spend time together
I know she misses me
And remembers me everyday.

I thought I could never have that someone...

She who thinks of me always
She who still loves me despite my flaws
She who wants to be with me the most.

I am blessed I got that someone.
And that someone is
She who calls me mama.

When Could I be Like a Butterfly

Loraine Garcia Asas

Of years that passed
Couldn't make me tough
As I started to get away at once
All I found was myself
Going back from the start.

I may not be holding that transcending beauty
Neither have a refined quality
But somehow, I believe in the majestic powers of dream
Still I believe
Still I dream.

In His gracious hands, I am entrusting my dreams
I wish I could have such flamboyant wings
Like those of a butterfly
Which is free to fly high
When could I be like a butterfly?

Someday I can get out from this
From my cocoon, I will come out
And like a metamorphosing butterfly,
I will flap my wings
And go further to reach the sky
And when I fly down,
I will go back to the garden of life
Where butterflies could cry.

Through

Loraine Garcia Asas

And now their tears keep falling

I've never seen this before

I don't have any choice

But to accept that everything's done

The control isn't mine

It's over now.

Here I am still wandering

No place to go

I try to run

Call out on someone

Wishing to be noticed

But no one can hear me

No one even bothers to look.

I try another step

But everything, everyone

Though they seem so close

Turn to be beyond my reach.

And I see everything from beginning to end

But it quickly vanishes

I cannot even utter their names

Everything, everyone seems so strange.

When Everyone Else Does

Loraine Garcia Asas

The clock ticks lazily

And I feel stuck between its little intervals

If only time will run fast

If only I can leave without turning back

I'd rather hide and rest in my own safe zone.

When everyone else does laugh inconsiderately

When everyone else does converse egoistically

When everyone else does look dreadfully

When everyone else doe smile sarcastically

When everyone else does everything freely

With no hesitation

With no consideration...

Is that just a matter of courage?

Of boldness?

Of attitude?

Of control?

Or simply a matter of upbringing?

The clock ticks lazily

And I feel stuck between its little intervals

If only time will run fast

If only I can leave without turning back

I'd rather hide and rest in my own safe zone

When everyone else does.

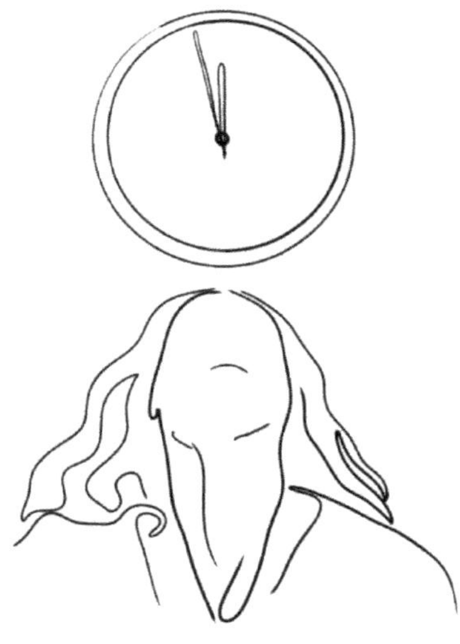

The Image that Stays in the Mirror

Loraine Garcia Asas

Some can easily define you
As if they know you
Telling you are like this
Or you are like that
As if they really know you
More than you know yourself.

Some will look at you
From your head to toe
Some will do the reverse
And others will do both
Then you will realize
It is awkward to be in that situation.

Does the image you see in the mirror
Differ from the image they can see in you?
Does the image you see in the mirror
Suddenly change when they stare at you?

It is easy to judge
Most of the time, the tongue slips fast
That it becomes too late before they realize
That they don't know you
That they have no idea, even a little
Of the war you have with yourself.

Some will look at you
From your head to toe
Some will do the reverse
And others will do both...

I'm Dead

Lorela Garcia Carpio

I passed by the school gate
'twas exactly six fifty-eight
I greeted the school guard with a smile
But didn't get the usual greeting all the while.

I walked fast through the pathway
Looking at flood water from left and right
Saw the gardener and said 'good day!'
But got no response that makes my day.

I got into the stairs to log in for attendance
My colleagues were also there
But no one bothered to glance
'twas fine I swear.

I got downstairs and headed to our room
My colleagues seemed to have faced the doom
No one spoke to me and I wondered why
I shrugged my shoulders and thought they may
be shy.

I hurriedly walked straight to my class
Surprised by a teacher wearing an eyeglass
I stepped back so she won't see
While verifying if that class wasn't for me.

I stayed at our usual corner
Waiting for the first period class to finish
It was like waiting for eternity
While the time elapsed from me.

I saw corridors filled with students out from their classrooms
Like the meadows beaming white with blooming mushrooms
I saw an angel through the light where I was being led
It was only then that I knew I'm dead.

Journey to Sta. Lucia

Lorela Garcia Carpio

At quarter to three
My alarm clock reminds me
To get up and prepare for my journey.

Everyday, as if by a stroke of fate
I battle with time so as not to be late
And beat the bell as I step into the gate.

Through quite a long while
I traverse the countless mile
Of an exhausting journey
Through an old rusty jeepney.

And everyday, I see the world in a different view
With stories of old and new
Unfathomable, for me and you.

For each moment in the jeepney
I hear fragment of a story
Sometimes happy, oftentimes weary.

Wonder what I see?
Faces masked for secrecy
And behaviors coated with honey.

With what I smell
Well, not all is well
There are colognes and perfumes that can ring the bell
There are also scents that we cannot tell.

As for the feeling it's always bothersome
For I'm certain that to be left alone will come
And all I have to do is to remain calm.

Then at one point, I'll leave the jeepney
To find a trike and continue my journey
Through a road of potholes and beauty.

Whenever I look back
To the place where mysticism thrive and flock
I remember my journey to a quagmire
That holds both paradise and fire.

My CWD

Lorela Garcia Carpio

Because of him I'm always glad

There's no minute or second that I feel bad

Whenever he's around, my gloom vanishes

And my heart overflows with positive wishes.

He may not be like any other
I know he's different and special

People around look at him with suppressed laughter

But his disability for me is trivial.

He can hardly move around all day
But he tries his best to run and play

He greets me every morning with a charming gaze

And bids me good night with his head bumping craze.

Yes, he wiggles when he walks

And sounds harder when he talks

He is just fond of sitting on the sofa

And waits for his food strips of salmon and tuna.

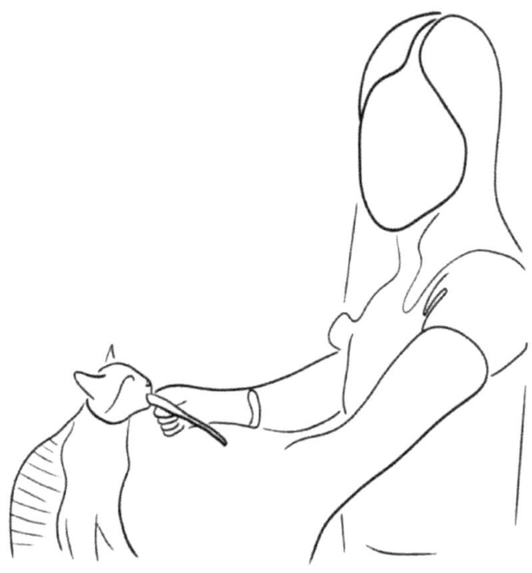

Maybe he'd stumble a hundred times

Because of his legs that wobble like chimes

He would pursue to jump and always fall

It's his persistence that I love most of all.

He may not be one whom everyone would care about

Nor one who would receive “I love you” with a shout

But he is the best companion that I ever had

The ‘Cat with Disability’ that makes me glad.

"That is part of the beauty of all
literature.
You discover that your longings
are universal longings,
that you're not lonely and
isolated from anyone.
You belong."
-F. Scott Fitzgerald

ABOUT THE AUTHORS

LORELA GARCIA CARPIO has been an English teacher for 27 years now.

She has earned her Complete Academic Requirements (CAR) for the degree Doctor of Philosophy in English Language and Literature (Ph.D.-ELL) from La Consolacion University Philippines where she obtained her Master of Arts in Education, major in English (MAE-English) as *magna cum laude*.

She is currently in the service of Department of Education- Sta. Lucia National High School as a Master (MT I) handling literature and research subjects.

LORAINE GARCIA ASAS had been a college instructor handling Communication Arts and Literature subjects at the Immaculate Conception International College of Arts and Technology.

She obtained her degree, Bachelor of Arts in Mass Communication, major in Broadcasting (AB-Broadcasting) at Bulacan State University.

She has earned her Complete Academic Requirements (CAR) for the degree, Master in Public Administration major in Fiscal Administration (MPA-Fiscal Administration) from La Consolacion University Philippines.

She is currently connected with the Regional Trial Court of Caloocan City as Court Interpreter III.

LORELA GARCIA CARPIO and LORAINE GARCIA ASAS were recognized as Best Writers 2023 in the International Ophir & Poetry Planet Awards for Writers for their book, Off to Beyond.

www.ingramcontent.com/pod-product-compliance
Lightning Source LLC
LaVergne TN
LVHW050330160826
845677LV00014B/3584

* 9 7 8 6 2 1 4 9 5 2 6 6 3 *